WHEN THE MOON WAS BLUE

and other stories

CLIVEDEN PRESS

Published in Great Britain in 1994 by Cliveden Press,
an imprint of Egmont Publishing Limited, Egmont House,
PO Box 111, Great Ducie Street, Manchester M60 3BL.
Printed in Finland

ISBN 0 7498 2039 X

Enid Blyton

Enid Blyton was born in London in 1897. Her childhood was spent in Beckenham, Kent, and as a child she began to write poems, stories and plays. She trained to be a teacher but she devoted her whole life to being a children's author. Her first book was a collection of poems for children, published in 1922. In 1926 she began to write a weekly magazine for children called *Sunny Stories*, and it was here that many of her most popular stories and characters first appeared. The magazine was immensely popular and in 1953 it became *The Enid Blyton Magazine*.

She wrote more than 600 books for children and many of her most popular series are still published all over the world. Her books have been translated into over 30 languages. Enid Blyton died in 1968.

Contents

When the moon was blue 7

Jane goes out to stay 32

"It's my birthday" 41

The Tom Thumb fairies 50

Midnight tea party 60

The big black cat 62

The goat, the duck, the goose and the cock 70

Conceited Clara 80

Mother Hubbard's honey 87

When the moon was blue

One evening, when Jack and Mary were going to bed, they forgot to clean their teeth. Mummy saw their toothbrushes lying beside their tooth-mugs and called to them.

"You naughty children! You haven't cleaned your teeth!"

"We forgot!" said Jack, and the two ran to get their brushes. "Have you ever forgotten to clean your teeth, Mummy?"

"Oh, I daresay I have," said Mummy.

"How often?" asked Mary.

"Oh, once in a blue moon!" said their Mummy, drawing back the curtains so that the air could come into the room.

"What's a blue moon?" said Jack.

"I really don't know," said Mummy.

7

"Just an ordinary moon turned blue, I expect. I've never seen one."

"You often say things happen 'once in a blue moon'," said Mary. "But a blue moon never comes."

"Well – it might some day!" laughed Mummy. "You'd better be careful then – for goodness knows what might happen if the moon turned blue!"

The children got into bed. Mummy kissed them and said goodnight. Then she turned out the light and went downstairs.

"It's very light out of doors tonight," said Mary. "The moon must be up."

"Daddy said it would be a full moon tonight," said Jack. "Oh, Mary – wouldn't it be exciting if it was blue!"

"Yes, but it won't be," said Mary sleepily. "Things like that never seem to happen. Think how often we've tried to see fairies and never have – and how often we've wished wishes and they haven't come true – and tried to work spells and they won't work. I don't believe in those things any more!"

"I still do," said Jack, "because once one of my wishes really did come true."

"Well, it must have been an accident, then," said Mary, yawning. "Goodnight, Jack. I'm going to sleep."

Both children fell fast asleep in a minute or two. They slept soundly, and didn't hear the wardrobe creaking loudly. They didn't hear the cat mewing outside either.

But when twelve o'clock struck, they did hear something. At least Jack did. He heard an owl hooting outside the window, and he opened his eyes.

"Wit-wit!" said the owl, "woo-wit-wit!"

Jack sat up and wondered what time it was. He looked at the window. A good deal of light came in from outside, for the moon was full. It had gone behind a cloud for a moment, quite a small one, for Jack could see the moon skimming along behind it. He watched it, waiting for it to come out again.

And when it did he gasped and stared

and rubbed his eyes – for what do you suppose? Why, the big round moon was as blue as forget-me-nots! There it shone in the sky, looking very peculiar indeed.

"There's a blue moon!" cried Jack. "Mary, Mary, wake up! There's a blue moon!"

Mary woke up with a jump and sat up. She stared at the moon in the greatest surprise.

"So there is!" she said. "Oh, Jack – do you suppose anything extraordinary will happen? Oh, do let's go to the window and see if we can spy any fairies or pixies about. Mummy said we might see them once in a blue moon!"

They ran to the window – and looked down their moonlit garden. But not a fairy or pixie could they see.

"Let's wish a few wishes!" said Jack, gazing up at the bright blue moon. "They might come true now the moon is blue."

"Yes, let's," said Mary. "I wish we could see a fairy or a gnome or something!"

"And I wish we could, too!" said Jack.

And immediately they did! A gnome, very small and bent, ran out from under the lilac bush in the middle of the garden, and went to the little round pool. In the middle of this was a little statue of a bunny, sitting on a big flat stone.

The gnome jumped over the water and landed beside the bunny. At once the stone rabbit took his hand and stood up. The gnome began to pull at the flat stone on which the bunny had been sitting – and before the children's very eyes, he suddenly disappeared! The stone bunny sat down again and made no movement.

"Did you see that, Mary?" cried Jack. "Come on, quickly! We'll see where he disappeared to. Put on your dressing-gown and I'll put on mine."

They threw on their dressing-gowns

and ran quietly down the stairs. Out they went into the garden and ran to the pond. With a leap Jack was over the water and standing beside the stone bunny in the middle of the pond. To his enormous surprise, the small rabbit at once put a cold paw into his hand and got up. Jack turned to the flat stone – and saw an iron ring on it, and the stone came up. Under it lay a steep stone stairway!

"Come on, Mary!" cried Jack. "Here's an adventure for us! We've always wanted one!"

Mary jumped over the water beside Jack, and peered down the steps. The stone rabbit put its other paw into her hand, and looked beseechingly at her.

"This little rabbit's alive, although it's just a statue!" said Mary, in surprise. "Can you speak, Bunny?"

"Yes," said the rabbit. "I can speak once in a blue moon – and the moon is blue tonight!"

"Are you really a statue or are you alive?" asked Jack.

"I was once the first rabbit in the carriage of the Princess Philomela of Heylo Land," said the bunny. "But one night the wicked gnome Twisty lay in wait for her carriage – and put a log in our path. So over I went and all the other three rabbits, and the Princess fell out of the carriage. The gnome picked her up and carried her off – and turned me and the other rabbits into stone. He sold us for the middles of ponds and there we stayed!"

"Goodness me!" said Jack, in the greatest surprise. "Whoever would have thought of such a thing? Where is the Princess now?"

"I don't know," said the rabbit, mournfully. "She's still a prisoner somewhere, I expect. The gnome has a secret way to Fairyland down that stairway. He may have gone to the Princess now."

"Well, let's go after him then!" said

Jack. "We may see where he keeps the Princess, and perhaps be able to rescue her! Will you come with us, Bunny?"

"Yes, but I'm made of stone, and I would make so much noise!" said the rabbit.

"I'll wish you alive again!" said Jack. "It seems as if wishes come true once in a blue moon!"

"Yes, wish!" said Mary. So Jack wished hard.

"I wish this stone bunny may come alive!" he said – and immediately his wish came true! The little rabbit grew soft and warm and furry – and whiskers grew out of his cheeks. The stone bunny had had no whiskers at all.

"I'm alive. I'm alive!" he cried, frisking round and nearly falling into the pond.

"Mind! You'll fall in the water!" said Mary, clutching hold of the excited bunny. "Come along. We'll go down the steps now."

So down the steps they all went, Jack first, then the bunny, then Mary. It was dark when they got to the bottom, but a lamp hung a little way farther on, and showed them a narrow passage. They went along, most excited.

After a while they came to a turnstile, and they pushed against it. It wouldn't turn round, and Jack thought they had better climb over it. But before he could do so, a small brownie popped his head out of a window in the wall of the passage and said: "Penny each, please."

"We haven't any pennies," said Jack. "We are in our dressing-gowns, and we don't keep pennies there. Please let us through. Has the Twisty Gnome gone this way?"

"Yes, he has," said the brownie, nodding his head. "He often goes this way. No one else goes, except myself – and I only go once in a blue moon!"

"Well, it's a blue moon tonight!" said Jack. "We've seen it!"

"What!" cried the brownie, his face full of excitement. "The moon is blue! My stars, I must go and look!"

He squeezed himself through the window in the wall of the passage, pushed past Jack, Mary and the rabbit and disappeared up the tunnel.

"Come on, let's climb over, now he's gone!" said Mary. So they all climbed over the turnstile, and went on down the tunnel again. But it didn't go very far this time. It opened out into a cave through which a dark, swift river ran. A little pixie sat by the side of some boats, half-asleep.

"Wake up!" cried Jack, running to him. "Has the Twisty Gnome gone this way?"

"Yes, down the river," said the pixie, in surprise. "But he said I was to let no one else but him have my boats today."

"Oh, well, it can't matter once in a blue moon!" said Jack, getting into one.

"What, is the moon blue?" cried the pixie, in delight. "Oh, have my boats then, have them all if you want to! I'm going up to see the moon, the moon, the moon!"

He sat down on a big toadstool growing nearby, and, to the children's great amazement, shot upwards at a great speed.

"Well, I suppose he's gone to see the moon, like the brownie," said Jack. "Come on, Mary and Bunny! We mustn't let the Twisty Gnome get too far ahead!"

They set off in the boat. Jack steered, but there was no need for oars, for the river was very strong and took them along itself. In a few minutes it came out into the open air, and there, hanging in the sky, was the moon, still as blue as forget-me-nots!

As the boat went along, Jack caught sight of a large notice on one of the banks. He looked at it. To his great surprise, it had one word on it:

JUMP!

"Jump," said Jack, puzzled; "why jump?"

"Oh, look!" cried Mary, pointing

ahead. "There is a waterfall or something coming. Jack, if we don't jump, we shall go over the falls. Oh, I'm frightened!"

"Come with me," the bunny said. He took the strings from Jack and pulled the boat towards the bank. It ran into it with a bump, and at the same time all three jumped out! They landed on the soft grass and rolled over. Just ahead of them the river shot over the falls with a roar. Their boat spun round once and then headed for the waterfall. Over it went, and that was the last they saw of it!

"Goodness! I hope this sort of thing only happens once in a blue moon!" said Jack.

"Oh, it does," said the bunny. "Come on. Do you see that castle over there? I am sure that is where the gnome has gone. It belongs to him. Perhaps he has the Princess Philomela locked up in one of the rooms."

They all set off for the castle. They

soon arrived there, and looked up at it. It was very big, and had hundreds of windows, and a great wooden door.

"I don't think I want to go in that door," said Mary. "It looks as if it might shut behind us and make us prisoners in the castle, too. Isn't there another way of getting in?"

"We'll spy round and see," said Jack. So they walked all round the castle – and right at the back they discovered a very small door, painted a bright yellow. Jack pushed it – and it came open!

He and the others peeped inside. It led into a great yard. They all went inside and looked round. The kitchen door stood open and a smell of cakes being baked came out.

"Come on," said Jack. "We may be able to sneak inside."

He crept up to the kitchen door – and at that moment a large gnome-woman came to it to shake a duster. She stared at the three in surprise. They didn't know what to say.

"Oh," she said at last. "I suppose you have come with a message for the Twisty Gnome. You are not the washing, are you? Or the baker?"

"Oh, no!" said Jack. "May we go inside and see the gnome?"

Mary was horrified to hear Jack ask this, for she certainly didn't want to see the horrid Twisty Gnome, in case they were all taken prisoners. The gnome servant nodded her head.

"He's just upstairs with the Princess," she said. "But he won't be long. Come and wait in the hall."

She took them inside and led them to a great hall. They sat down on a bench and she disappeared back into the kitchen.

"Did you hear that?" said Jack. "She said the Twisty Gnome was upstairs with the Princess! So she *is* here! We'll rescue her! Come on – we must hide before the gnome comes back. I don't want to see him, of course – that was only an excuse to get inside!"

Jack, Mary and the rabbit looked round to see where they could hide. There was a long curtain hanging at the foot of the stairs, and the three crept behind it. They hadn't been there more than a minute or two when they heard footsteps coming down the stairs. It was the Twisty Gnome.

As he came into the hall, the gnome-woman ran out. "Master," she said, "there are three . . ."

She stopped short and looked round in surprise – for she could not see Mary, Jack or the bunny. "How strange!" she said. "A boy and a girl and a rabbit came to see you. They were here just now!"

"Oh, indeed!" said Twisty, in a hoarse and threatening voice. "They were here, were they? Well, where are they now? I suppose you've let them go into my magic room, and disturb my spells. Grrrrrr! If you have, I'll turn you into a dustbin lid. That's all you're fit for!"

"Oh, Master, I don't think they've gone into your magic room!" cried the servant – but the gnome had disappeared into a little room on the opposite side of the hall. The servant followed – and in a trice Mary, Jack and the rabbit slipped out from the curtain and were running upstairs as fast as they could.

At each landing there was a locked door. Jack stopped outside each one and called softly.

"Princess Philomela! Are you there?"

But there was no reply at all until he reached the topmost room of all – and then an answer came, in a soft, eager voice.

"Yes, yes! I am here! Who is it?"

The door was locked and bolted – but the key was in the lock. Jack turned it, and then undid the bolts. He opened the door – and saw inside the room a beautiful little princess with long golden hair waving round her face, and the brightest blue eyes he had ever seen.

"Oh, oh, you've come to rescue me!"

cried Philomela, and she gave Jack and Mary a tight hug each. She saw the bunny and clapped her hands in delight.

"Why, you are dear little Whiskers, one of the bunnies that used to pull my carriage!" she said, and she lifted him up and kissed him. "I suppose you brought these children here to save me."

"We must go, Princess," said Jack. "The gnome knows we are here. He is looking for us downstairs. He may come up at any minute."

"Come along then," said Philomela.

So they all began to creep down the stairs and at last came to the hall. No one was there. Not a sound was to be heard. Every door that led into the hall was shut.

"I say!" said Jack. "I don't remember which door led into the kitchen, do you?"

"We don't need to go that way," said Mary. "What about trying the front door?"

"No," said Jack. "It's too big and

heavy. It would make a noise. Let's go into one of the rooms; it doesn't much matter which one so long as the gnome isn't there, and then climb out of the window. That should be easy."

So they listened outside the nearest door, and, not hearing the tiniest sound from inside, they pushed open the door and slipped into the room. They ran to some curtains and pulled them aside to get at the windows – but alas – there were no windows at all!

Then they heard the sound of a key being turned in the lock – and looked round to see the Twisty Gnome looking at them with a very nasty grin.

"Ha!" he said. "So you thought you would rescue the Princess and all escape very nicely, did you? Well, you made a mistake, I'm afraid. I have four prisoners now, instead of one!"

He went to the middle of the floor, and pulled up a small wooden trap-door.

"Get down into my cellar," he said. "There is no escape from there. It is

dark and cold and full of spiders. You will enjoy a night or two there, I am sure!"

The Princess began to cry. Jack and Mary looked fierce, but could do nothing. The bunny slipped down into the cellar without a word.

When they were all in the dark, damp cellar, the gnome shut the trap-door with a bang and bolted it. They heard his footsteps going out of the room above.

"What are we going to do?" sobbed Philomela. "Oh, I am so frightened."

"So am I!" said Mary, wiping her eyes.

"There's no need to be," said the rabbit, in a soft voice. "I can rescue you all. I am a bunny, you know, and my paws are good for digging holes. This cellar is in the ground – there is earth all around. It will not take me long to dig my way out. Then I will fetch many more rabbits and we will all dig together."

"Splendid idea!" cried Jack. The

rabbit at once began to scrape in the earth. Soon he had made quite a tunnel, and the earth was piled in the cellar. In a few minutes he had disappeared – and before long he had fetched fifteen more rabbits, who all dug and scraped away valiantly.

"Now I think the tunnel is big enough," said the rabbit. And so it was. Jack, Mary and Philomela easily made their way up it, and came out at the side of the big castle!

"The rabbits have brought a carriage for you, Your Highness," said the little bunny – and there, sure enough, was a shining silver carriage! Four rabbits stood ready to pull it, and the Princess got in.

"You must come, too," she said to the children – but just as they were about to get in, a peculiar thing happened.

"Look at the moon!" cried the rabbit, and pointed to where the moon was slowly sinking down the sky.

Everyone looked. It was turning

bright yellow! Yes – there was no mistake about it. All its blue colour was fading – and even as they watched, it was all gone, and there was the moon, as bright yellow as a daffodil, filling the sky with light.

"The blue moon's gone," said the rabbit sadly. "It's gone – but we've rescued the Princess!"

A strange wind blew up at that moment and the children suddenly felt giddy. There came a loud humming noise. Jack and Mary sat down on the grass and shut their eyes, for they felt very strange.

After a while the humming noise died away – and they opened their eyes.

Will you believe it? They were back in their beds again! Yes, they were – both of them sitting up and gazing out of the window at the moon, which was yellow, and shining brightly!

"Mary!" cried Jack. "Did we dream it all?"

"No, we couldn't have," said Mary. "It

was all so real. The moon really *was* blue!"

"Well, tomorrow we will look for that trap-door again, where the bunny was," said Jack, lying down. "Then we will know for certain it was all true. How funny – Daddy will wonder where the stone bunny is gone, won't he?"

But do you know, when the morning came, the stone bunny was back again. Yes, he was – standing in the middle of the pond on the big flat stone just as before.

"But the trap-door is underneath him, Daddy," said Mary, earnestly, after she had told Daddy all about their very strange adventure. "It really is. Will you take him off the stone and see?"

"No," said Daddy. "He is cemented to the stone. I'm not going to move him. You dreamt it all!"

Well, isn't that a pity? If only Daddy would move the rabbit, and let the children find that trap-door again, they would know that it wasn't a dream. But Daddy won't.

Perhaps *you* will see a blue moon one day. If you do, wish a wish – for it is sure to come true, once in a blue moon!

Jane goes out to stay

Jane was going to stay with her friend Pam. She felt very grown-up indeed. She had never been away from home before – but here she was, watching Mummy pack a little bag with her nightdress and dressing-gown, her flannel, sponge and toothbrush, and a clean dress.

"Shall I pack Bunny for you?" said Mummy.

"Oh, *no*," said Jane. "I know he sleeps with me every night, Mummy, but I'm too big to take a bunny away with me. Pam would laugh at me."

"No, she wouldn't. Pam is a year younger than you are, and I expect she takes a toy to bed with her every

single night," said Mummy. "Very well. I won't put Bunny in."

Jane thought of all the things she would tell Pam. She wanted to make Pam think she was very grown-up and important. She would say, "Pam, do you know this – Pam, do you know that?" and Pam would listen eagerly.

She arrived at Pam's in time for dinner. Pam hugged her, because she liked Jane very much.

"Do you mind being away from home?" she said. "Will you like staying with me? I've never stayed away even one night without Mummy."

"Ah, but I'm older than you," said Jane. "I'm in a class higher at school, too. I shan't mind staying away from home a bit!"

They had dinner, and then they went out to play. The dog next door barked, and made Pam jump.

"Are you afraid of dogs?" said Jane. "I've got a dog of my own at home. Can you ride?"

"No, I can't. Can you?" asked Pam.

"Oh, yes. I ride every Saturday, on a big, white pony called Sweetie," said Jane. "I gallop. And once I went so fast that everyone thought my pony was running away. But he wasn't."

"You must be very clever," said Pam. "I wish I could do things like that."

Jane chose all the games, and she chose ones she was quite the best in. She could run faster than Pam, and she could jump higher.

"Mummy, Jane is wonderful," said Pam, when they went in to tea. "She does everything so well. And she's not a bit afraid of dogs or horses – or of tigers, either, are you, Jane?"

"I don't expect I would be, if I met one," said Jane, pleased at all this praise. "I like animals. You ought to like animals, too, Pam, then you wouldn't be so scared when you see a big dog, or hear a cow moo."

After tea they played card games. Jane was much quicker at them than

Pam. She 'Snapped' everything, and won four games straight off. Pam looked a little sad.

"I wish I could win once," she said.

"Have a game of Happy Families. You may win then," said her mother, feeling rather sorry for the smaller girl. She thought that Jane might just let Pam win once, to please her. But no, Jane won Happy Families, too.

"I'm stupid, aren't I?" said poor Pam, almost in tears. "I wish I was as wonderful as Jane, Mummy. She can do everything. Jane, do you ever cry?"

"Oh, no," said Jane. But this wasn't quite true. She did cry sometimes.

"Not even when you fall down and hurt your knee?" asked Pam.

"Of *course* not!" said Jane.

"Are you ever frightened in the night?" said Pam. "Because I am."

"Of *course* I'm not," said Jane, in a scornful voice. "I just go to sleep, and don't bother about anything, not even thunder."

"You're too good to be true, Jane, dear," said Pam's Mummy. "And now I think it's bedtime. Hurry up and have a nice hot bath, because it's very cold tonight."

Soon the two little girls were in separate little beds, drinking a nice warm glass of milk. Then Pam's mother said good night to them both, and went downstairs.

She came up a little later with Pam's hot water bottle, and one for Jane, too. But Jane was already fast asleep. So very gently Pam's mother pushed the hot water bottle, in its soft furry cover, down into the bed beside the sleeping Jane. Jane never had a hot water bottle at home, and had not asked for one.

About three hours later Jane woke up. She felt a warm patch against her legs. Whatever could it be? She put down her hand and felt it. It was soft and furry and warm. It must be some animal that had crept into bed with her when she was asleep!

"Go away!" said Jane, and kicked out at it. But it didn't move. It just lay against her leg, furry and warm. Jane felt suddenly frightened.

She sat up in bed and shouted. "Help! Help! There's a wild animal in bed with me! It's biting me, it's biting me, help, help!"

Pam woke up with a jump. She switched on the light and stared at Jane. "Oh, Pam! There's a horrid wild animal in bed with me!" cried Jane again. "It'll bite me to bits! I believe it's nibbling me now! Oh! OHHHHH!"

"I'll save you, I'll save you!" cried Pam, and she jumped out of bed. She pulled Jane right out of bed, and then threw back the covers. She saw the furry hot water bottle cover, and bent to pick it up and throw it away, thinking it was some animal.

Then she saw what it was. How she stared! Then she laughed. She had a very merry little laugh, that went ha-ha-ha-ho-ho-ho, he-he. She rolled on

Jane's bed and she laughed till the tears came into her eyes.

"What's the matter, Pam?" asked Jane, upset. But Pam was laughing too much to tell her. Then in came Pam's mother to see what all the noise was about.

"Oh, Mummy, oh, Mummy! Jane was so funny!" said Pam. "She screamed and shouted and cried because she said she had a wild animal in her bed that was biting her to bits! And I got out to rescue her from the dreadful animal – and it was only her hot water bottle!"

Then it was Mummy's turn to laugh. "Well, well, well – to think of our brave and wonderful Jane being scared of a hot water bottle! I slipped it into your bed, dear, when you were asleep."

Poor Jane! She did feel so very, very silly. To think she had yelled like that over a hot water bottle.

She got back into bed, very red in the face. She threw the hot water bottle out on the floor.

"Now don't be cross as well as foolish, Jane," said Pam's mother. "It really was very funny, you know, and we couldn't help laughing. And don't you think little Pam was brave, to jump out of bed and come and try to save you from the wild animal you were shouting about?"

"Yes. She was brave," said Jane. "Thank you, Pam. You're braver than I am!"

Then they went to sleep. But you won't be surprised to hear that next day Jane was much nicer to Pam, and even let her win two games of Snap!

"It's my birthday"

J ib the brownie hadn't a proper house. He lived in a snug little tent that he had made out of the big leaves of the chestnut tree. He just sewed them together and, lo and behold, he had a nice little tent.

He used to live for a few days in one place and then roll up his tent, tie it on his back and go off to another village. And in every place he pitched his tent, he would say the same thing.

"It's my birthday tomorrow!"

Then he would sigh and look sad, and the people round him would say, "Why do you look sad?"

And Jib would say, "Well, it's sad to be away from home and my friends and have a birthday – no presents, no cards, nothing!"

Well, the pixies and elves were kind little people and you can guess what they did!

"Let's go and buy Jib birthday cards and some little presents!" they would say, and off they would go at once.

And the next day Jib would have lovely cards and all kinds of nice little presents. The little folk would beam at him and wonder if he would give a birthday party and ask them all to it.

But he never did. On that very afternoon he would quietly fold up his chestnut-leaf tent and steal away; and when a pixie came by, no Jib and no tent were there! That was really very mean of him.

One day he came to the village of Ho. It was full of brownies like himself, and pixies and elves. Jib put up his little tent, and people came to call.

"My name's Jib," he said. "I hope you don't mind my staying here in my tent.

It seems such a nice place and such nice people."

"Oh, we like to make strangers welcome," said Boff, a big, burly brownie with a very long beard. "We hope you'll be happy here."

Jib hung his head and looked sad. "I expect I *shall* be happy soon," he said, "but just now I feel rather miserable. You see – it's my birthday tomorrow – and it's sad to be far from home and have no cards and no presents."

"Dear me – we must do something about *that*," said kind Mrs Boff. She and Boff went off, talking together, and Jib grinned to himself. Now he would have plenty of cards and heaps of presents.

"I shall leave tomorrow afternoon, and go to Cherry Village and sell all the presents," he said to himself. "I shall get a nice lot of money for them. How very stupid people are, to be sure!"

Mr and Mrs Boff went round the village of Ho, telling everyone that Jib was having a birthday the next day and people must try and make it nice for him.

"Hm!" said Old Wily the goblin. "I don't much like the look of that fellow, Jib. Why should we spend money on him? Would he spend any on us?"

"Oh, he's sure to have a little party and ask us all to it," said Mrs Boff. "He'll be so pleased with his cards and presents, he'll surely want to do something nice in return."

Old Wily didn't think that a brownie with a mean face like Jib's would ever want to do anything nice for anyone. He sat and thought for a little while, and then he put on his old hat and went to visit his cousin, Old Sly. There wasn't much that Old Sly didn't know. He had lived a long time and he had heard a lot and knew a lot. He was two hundred years old and his beard had grown down to his feet and round his ankles.

"Ever heard of anyone called Jib?" asked Old Wily.

Old Sly frowned and thought for a

long while. "Ah, yes," he said at last. "He's the fellow who goes round with a chestnut-leaf tent and says he's miserable because it's his birthday and he's far from home. Then he collects a whole lot of presents and sells them in the next village. A very unpleasant fellow."

"Thank you, Old Sly," said Old Wily. "Exactly what I thought." Off he went back to the village of Ho, thinking hard. He found that everyone had bought a card or a present for Jib.

Old Wily went to visit the baker. "It's Mr Jib's birthday tomorrow," he said. "And he wants to have a nice little party. Will you arrange it, please? Birthday cake and buns and sandwiches and ice-creams and biscuits and jellies and balloons and crackers. All the very best, of course."

"Certainly, certainly," said the baker, delighted, and he set to work.

Well, next day Jib sat in his tent and waited for the little folk to bring him cards and presents. And as usual they did! Dear me, what a lot of money they had spent on that rascal Jib.

"So kind of you!" he kept saying. "So very kind! Thank you, thank you!"

"He hasn't said anything about a party yet," whispered Mrs Boff.

"Oh, there'll be a party," said Old Wily. "Yes, yes – there's sure to be a party. A fine one, too. I've seen the baker icing a splendid birthday cake."

Well, Jib heard this, as Old Wily meant that he should, and he was delighted. "What! A party as well as all these presents," he thought. "Magnificent!"

So he didn't fold up his chestnut-leaf tent and steal away as he usually did. He waited for the party!

It was a very fine party indeed. The birthday cake was made in the shape of a white palace and really looked lovely. Everyone had two pieces. Jib had three, and goodness knows how many cakes and buns and ice-creams he had as well.

And after the party, when everyone was saying goodbye, the baker came up and bowed. "I hope everything was all right, Mr Jib," he said.

"Perfectly," said Jib. "Couldn't be better."

"I'm glad," said the baker and unrolled a long sheet of paper. "Here's the bill."

What a bill it was! Jib stared in horror. What! All that money for a party. Well, *he* wasn't going to pay for it!

"I'm not paying that," he said, roughly.

"But it was *your* birthday party!" said Old Wily, who had put himself nearby. "Surely you gave it in return for the kindness of all these people? Surely, Jib, you didn't mean to fold up your tent and go without paying the bill? Oh, surely not! Where is Mr Plod the policeman? Let us ask him if that would be a right thing to do."

Jib looked very scared. He didn't like

48

policemen. He was always afraid they would find out all his mean little tricks. He hurriedly put his hand into his pocket, and pulled out a very fat purse. He paid the baker's bill without a word.

"That was wise of you, Jib, very wise," said Old Wily. "I hope you will *always* pay for birthday parties on the many birthdays you have each year. Will you, Jib?"

Jib began to tremble. He waited till everyone had gone then he packed up his tent quickly. Old Wily watched him go. "I'm coming to your next birthday party!" he called. "Let me see now – when is your next birthday, Jib? Next week, I suppose. I'll be there!"

Jib went hurrying off without a word, and so far as I know he hasn't had a birthday since! What a way to go on, wasn't it?

The Tom Thumb fairies

O nce upon a time there were some very small creatures called Tom Thumb fairies – so small that you could easily hold a hundred in the palm of your hand and hardly feel any weight.

They lived in some little red toadstools in Toadstool Village on the borders of Fairyland. The toadstools were small enough, goodness knows, but the fairies were so tiny that each toadstool was as big as a house to them. So they hung curtains at the windows in the top, and had a little door in the stalk with a knocker and a letter-box, just as you have.

Now one night there came a band of red goblins creeping round Toadstool

Village. It was a dark night and there were so many clouds that not even the stars gave their faint light. The goblin chief gave a signal, and at once two goblins went to each toadstool house, opened the door and captured the small fairy inside the bedroom at the top of the toadstool.

Nobody heard them squeal. Nobody heard them struggle. They were popped into bags and taken off to Goblin Town at once, there to wait on the goblins and help them with their spells. Their wings were clipped off, so that they could not fly home. The wings grew again in a few weeks' time, but every time they grew the goblins clipped them off again.

The Tom Thumb fairies were very unhappy. "What shall we do?" they wept. "We hate working underground all day long. We hate these red goblins, who are so unkind. We don't know the way home. We have no wings to fly with."

One day one of the Tom Thumb

fairies found a worm-hole leading up to the sunlight. She was overjoyed, and she whispered the news to the others.

"One morning when the goblins have gone off somewhere, we will creep up this worm-hole and escape," said the fairy.

"But the goblins will come after us," said the others. "We shan't know which way to go when we get up into daylight again."

"Never mind," said the first one. "We will see what we can do."

So the next time the red goblins went off together, leaving the Tom Thumb fairies to do all the work, the tiny creatures began to make their way up the worm-hole. It was very small – but they were smaller still.

Soon they came to the worm, and they could not get by, for the worm was fat and lay squeezed up in its bedroom – a large part of the hole halfway down the passage.

"Please move up a bit," said one of the

Tom Thumbs, poking the worm. "We want to get by."

The worm moved up its hole. It put out its head and listened, for it had no eyes to see with. Was any sharp-eyed bird about? No – it could hear no pattering of feet. So it drew itself right up and let the fairies use its rather slimy hole as a passage up to the daylight.

How pleased the Tom Thumbs were when they saw the bright sunshine again! "Now we must plan what to do," they cried.

"Get back into your hole," shouted a fairy to the worm. "The red goblins may come after us. Don't you move out of your hole for them, or they will catch us."

"There are plenty of other holes for the red goblins to come up by," said the worm, sliding back again. "There's the mouse-hole just over there – and the big rabbit-hole in the hedge – and any amount of empty worm-holes too."

"Oh dear!" said the Tom Thumbs, looking round as if they expected to see the red goblins at any moment. "We had better find a hiding-place in case they come. Where can we go?"

There were pink-tipped daisies about – much, much bigger than the Tom Thumb fairies. There was a large dandelion plant too, with great golden blossoms.

"I will hide you," said the dandelion in a soft silky voice. "You are so tiny that you can each slip under one of my many golden petals. Hurry now, for I can hear the red goblins coming."

In a trice the Tom Thumbs had run to the large dandelion, which spread its hundreds of soft petals to the sun. Each fairy lifted up a silken petal and slipped underneath. There they hid in safety whilst the red goblins, suddenly appearing from the mouse-hole, began to hunt for the Tom Thumbs.

"They must be somewhere about,"

shouted the chief one. "Hunt well, all of you."

Well, they hunted and they hunted, but no one thought of looking in the dandelion-head. There the Tom Thumbs hid, and did not make a movement for fear of being found.

"Well, goblins, we must get back to our home underground," said the chief at last. "But you, Gobo, and you, Feefo, and you, Huggo, stay up here and keep watch, in case those Tom Thumbs are hiding anywhere."

The goblins went back down the mouse-hole, but Gobo, Feefo and Huggo stayed behind, their sharp black eyes looking round and about. The Tom Thumbs did not dare to move.

"Don't you worry," whispered the dandelion. "You have a soft bed – and if you look hard you will find honey to eat, and when the night comes you will have dew to drink. Keep still and rest, and you will be safe."

Day after day the Tom Thumbs lay

hidden in the golden dandelion, whilst the three goblins kept a strict watch. The dandelion grew on its stalk and lifted the Tom Thumbs higher – and then something odd happened.

It was time for the golden dandelion-head to fade. The gold left it – it closed up like a bud once more, holding the Tom Thumbs safely inside. It was no longer a wide golden flower, but a rather untidy-looking dead one, tightly shut. It drooped its head so low that it hid it amongst the leaves. Still the Tom Thumbs lay hidden – because now they could not get out!

What would happen to them? They did not know. The honey was almost finished, and the dew no longer fell on to them for drink. They huddled together in the dead flower, frightened and miserable.

The stalk of the dandelion grew longer and longer. How strange! But it had a reason. Yes – for the flower was turning into seed – and when that seed was ready it must be taken up into the air on a long, long stalk so that the wind might blow it away. Oh, clever dandelion!

So it came about that one day the dead dandelion raised its head again, on its long, long stalk. It stood straight up once more, and – wonder of wonders! – instead of a golden head it now had a head full of marvellous white seeds. It was a beautiful dandelion clock.

And now the Tom Thumb fairies began to get excited. "Look!" they cried. "The dandelion has grown us little parachutes! Do look! There is one for each of us. We can hold on to the stalk – it is like a handle for us – and when the wind blows, the parachute of hairs will carry us far, far away from here, safe from the red goblins."

But the wind did not blow them away – someone else did. Who was that? Well, it may have been you! A little girl came down that way and saw the dandelion clock standing there, so tall and beautiful. She did not see the three red goblins still keeping a sharp watch. She picked the dandelion clock and looked at it.

"I shall blow you," she said. "I want to know the time. Now then – PUFF! – one o'clock. PUFF! – two o'clock. PUFF! – three o'clock. PUFF! – four o'clock. PUFF! – five o'clock. Oh, it's tea-time! I must hurry."

She ran off, pleased to see the pretty seeds blowing in the air – but she didn't see that each one carried a Tom Thumb fairy.

The dandelion seeds flew high and far. When at last they came to the ground they were far, far away from the red goblins' home. The Tom Thumbs took the first bus home they could find; and now they are safe in Toadstool Village again – and at night they all lock and bolt their doors!

Wasn't it lucky for them that they hid in a dandelion?

Midnight tea party

I peeped one night in the
   playroom,
And I was surprised to see
The pussycat and the teddy
Having their friends to tea!

The clockwork mouse and old Jumbo,
The sailor doll and the clown,
And all the dolls from the dolls' house
At the table were sitting down.

Pussy had borrowed my tea set,
And Teddy was cutting a cake,
There were jellies a-shake in the dishes,
And crackers for each one to take.

You think I was dreaming? I wasn't!
Today I found crumbs on the mat,
And jelly in one of the dishes,
And the pussycat's blue paper hat!

The big black cat

The big black cat from across the road used to sit on the wall and wait for Joan and Richard to come back from school.

He stood up and arched his back when he saw them coming. They ran up to him and stroked him, tickling his soft neck.

"You're a very nice cat," said Joan. "If you come into our garden this afternoon I'll give you a bit of fish. We're having fish for dinner, so there's sure to be a bit of skin for you off our plates."

The cat strolled into their garden almost every day. Sometimes the children gave him milk or little tit-bits. Sometimes they played with him, and

once he even went to sleep in Joan's doll's pram. That made Mummy laugh.

"Just look at that cat!" she said. "Anyone would think he belonged to you two children, not to Mrs Brown across the road."

The cat loved playing with the children's toys. He played ball very well. He liked running after Richard's clockwork train. He patted all the little dolls that sat in the train when they went for a ride.

Whenever he saw the children playing he went out to play with them. "Hallo, Blackie!" they would say, when he strolled into the garden. "Come along and play!"

But one day Richard played with something that Blackie couldn't catch or chase. He had a new aeroplane!

It was a lovely thing. It really could fly beautifully. It had to be wound up tightly with elastic, and then Richard held it high in the air, gave it a push off, and away it flew, whirring like a real aeroplane through the air. Sometimes it flew right down to the bottom of the garden.

The cat watched the aeroplane flying. It thought it must be some kind of toy bird. When it fell to the ground the cat went racing over to it, and pawed at it to make it fly again. But it wouldn't, of course, till Richard had wound up the elastic once more.

One day Richard flew the aeroplane when there was a very strong wind. It flew right up into the air and landed by the chimney. And there it stayed!

"Oh, dear," said Joan. "Look, Richard – it won't come back."

"It's stuck," said Richard, in dismay. "We must get a ladder."

But no ladder was long enough to reach up to the roof. Richard threw up a stick to try and dislodge the aeroplane, but Joan stopped him.

"No, don't do that – if the stick hits it, it will break a wing off the aeroplane

– and then it will never, never fly again."

"Well, what are we to do, then – leave it up there for ever and ever?" said Richard, sadly. He took a step backwards and trod on Blackie, who had been watching all this with great interest. Why didn't the aeroplane come back? Why did it like being up on the roof so much? Was there a bird's nest up there?

Blackie squealed when Richard trod on him. He bent down at once. "Oh, sorry, Blackie. Did I hurt you? I didn't see you there."

"Mee-ow," said Blackie, meaning that it didn't matter. He strolled up to a tree and sharpened his claws. Then up the tree he went in a bound, and on to the garage roof. He stopped to give himself a little wash, while he thought of what to do next.

Then he leapt up to the next roof, which led to the chimneys. Joan and Richard saw him.

"Look," said Joan. "Blackie's on the roof. I do hope he doesn't fall. I don't believe he's ever been on a roof before."

Blackie hadn't. He walked very carefully indeed. He climbed up the tiles to the chimney near to where the aeroplane rested. He came to it and sniffed at it.

"Blackie!" yelled Richard. "Blackie, be a clever cat – scrape at our aeroplane and get it down for us."

Blackie took no notice. He sniffed round, hoping to find a bird's nest. But there was none there, of course. He patted the aeroplane carefully. It moved just a little.

Blackie patted it again. He wanted it to fly as it usually did. Why wouldn't it? The wind came along and fluttered its tail. Blackie pounced on it. Up went the front part of the aeroplane as Blackie jumped at the tail, and the cat jumped back in alarm.

He nearly rolled down the tiles, but just managed to save himself. Joan squealed. Then Richard yelled loudly and made her jump.

"Look – Blackie has managed to get our aeroplane free – the wind's got it again – it's moving, it's moving!"

So it was! It slid down the roof a little way, and Blackie gave it a push. It slid all the way down the tiles with Blackie after it, came to the gutter, fell over it – and then glided down to earth through the air! It landed just by Richard.

"Oh, good cat, Blackie!" shouted Richard, in delight. "Clever cat! You've got my aeroplane back for me! Come down and we'll give you a treat!"

Blackie came down, pleased with himself. The children ran in and took some money from their money-box. Then they went to Mummy.

"Mummy," said Richard, "you've got some tins of sardines in your cupboard. Can we buy one for Blackie? He's just been very, very kind and good."

"Yes, if you like," said Mummy. "Whatever has he done?"

"He's climbed up on the roof, gone to the chimney, and set my aeroplane free for me," said Richard. "I really do think he deserves a treat."

Well, Blackie certainly enjoyed the sardines. He spent a whole hour afterwards washing himself. He wouldn't mind getting a dozen aeroplanes off the roof if he could have sardines as a reward!

And when the other cats smelt the sardine smell on him, and came round for a sniff, Blackie told them how he got such a treat – and, would you believe it, every time Joan and Richard fly that aeroplane now, at least half a dozen cats climb up to the roof and wait – just in *case* it gets stuck by the chimney again.

"I only hope it doesn't," says Richard, each time. "There wouldn't be much left of it if *all* those cats pounce on it to set it free!"

He needn't worry. Blackie will get there first!

The goat, the duck, the goose and the cock

Once upon a time there was a cock who was very tired of living with the hens in his yard, so he made up his mind to run away and find other friends. He set off one morning at dawn, and it wasn't long before he met a fine fat goose, walking along the lane.

"Good morning, Goose," said the cock. "Where are you off to?"

"I have lost my mistress, the goose-girl," said the goose. "I am seeking another mistress now."

"Come with me," said the cock, ruffling out his beautiful tail-feathers. "I am going to see the world."

So the goose and the cock walked on together. Presently they came to a little white duck waddling along as fast as her two unsteady legs would carry her.

"Good morning, Duck," said the cock. "Where are you off to?"

"I have heard bad news this morning," said the duck. "The red hen told me that my master was going to kill me for his supper. So I ran away, but I don't know where to go to."

"Come with us," said the cock, standing on his toes, and looking very grand. "We are going to see the world."

So the duck went with the goose and the cock, and they all walked down the lane together till they came to the common.

On the common was a billy-goat, and he had slipped the rope that tied him to his post, and was gambolling about free.

"Good morning," said the cock. "What are you going to do?"

"I don't know," said the goat, joyously. "I am free for the first time in my life – but I don't know where to go."

"Come with us," said the cock, making the red comb on his head stand up very high. "We are going to see the world."

So the goat went with the goose, the duck and the cock, and they all walked over the common together.

"What shall we do?" asked the goat.

"Shall we go to the town of Nottingham and stand by the roadside to beg?" said the cock. "I have a fine voice and I could sing for pennies."

"I could take round the hat," said the duck.

"I could clap my wings in time to your song," said the goose.

"And I could butt anyone who wouldn't give us a penny," said the goat.

So off they set for the town of Nottingham. When they got there it was market day and there were many people about. The four animals stood by

the side of the road, and the cock began to sing:

"Cock-a-doodle-doo,
My baby's lost her shoe,
It had a button blue,
What shall Baby do?"

The goose beat time with her wings, and the duck took round a hat for pennies. The goat stood by ready to butt anyone who would not give them anything.

But before the cock had quite finished his song a burly farmer came up.

"What's all this?" he cried. "Here are four creatures escaped from their pens. Catch them!"

Without waiting a moment the four animals ran away. Through the streets of Nottingham they went and found themselves on the hill outside the town.

"We were nearly caught!" said the goat. "We must not go near a town again. Whatever shall we do?"

"We had better find a cave to live in," said the cock. "See, there is one half-way up the hillside."

"A witch lives there with her ugly daughter," said the duck.

"We will go and ask her if there is another cave near by," said the goose. So off they all went. But when they got to the cave it was empty. No one was there. But there was a cupboard full of good things, and the hungry creatures had a good meal. Then they settled down to sleep.

Now that night the old witch and her daughter returned to the cave. They were a wicked couple, and the people of Nottingham had long tried to get rid of them. The witch stepped into the cave first, and lighted a candle – and the first thing she saw was the table, spread with the remains of the animals' meal.

"Someone has been here!" she cried, and stamped her foot. She and her daughter ran out of the cave and went to a nearby tree to think what they should do. They were afraid that an enemy was in the cave.

"Daughter, you creep back and find out," said the witch. "I will prepare a spell so that if any man or woman is in the cave they cannot harm you. Go."

Now when the witch had shouted and stamped her foot, the four animals had awakened in a fright. The goat was lying near the entrance of the cave, the goose was by the cupboard, the duck was under the table, and the cock was on the back of a chair. They waited to see if anything further would happen – and they heard the witch's daughter coming back.

"It's my mistress!" thought the goat.

"It's my master!" thought the duck.

"It's my mistress!" thought the cock.

"It's the goose-girl!" thought the goose. And all of them were frightened.

The witch's daughter came creeping in. She heard nothing at all. She went to the table and trod on one of the duck's feet underneath.

"Quack-quack, quack-quack-quack!" squawked the duck in pain, and dug his beak into the girl's leg. In a great fright she stumbled towards the cupboard and fell over the goose.

"Ss-ss-ss-ss-sss!" hissed the goose, and struck the witch's daughter with its great wings. Then it began to cackle loudly in fright. The girl was afraid and sat down in a chair trembling. But when she leaned back in the darkness she almost pushed the cock off the back of the chair, and he dug his claws into her hair in terror, crying "Cock-a-doodle-doo! Cock-a-doodle-doo!"

The witch's daughter could not bear it any longer. She fled to the entrance of the cave and fell right over the goat. He butted her so fiercely that she was sent rolling over and over down the hillside and only came to rest under the tree beside the witch.

"What is the matter?" cried the witch. "Didn't my spell work?"

"Oh Mother, oh Mother," said the

daughter, weeping. "The cave is full of powerful wizards. When I went in there was one under the table that cried 'Go back, go back!' And then he stuck a knife into my leg. By the cupboard is a snake that hissed at me in a dreadful manner, and then struck at me with its head. On the back of a chair sits another wizard who cried, 'What a rogue are you! What a rogue are you!' and then nearly pulled my hair out of my head. But worst of all is a giant wizard lying near the entrance. He flung me down the hillside, and here I am."

"What a dreadful thing!" said the witch, trembling. "Our sins have found us out. We must stay here no longer. Come, let us away before dawn."

They hurried off and no one ever heard of them again. As for the four animals, they soon fell asleep and slept peacefully till morning. When they awoke they looked round the cave and were pleased.

"We will live here together," said the cock. "No one will disturb us, for they think that this is a witch's home. We shall be happy here."

They settled down in peace together, and as far as I know, there they may be living still!

Conceited Clara

C lara was a doll – and goodness, what a marvellous doll she was! She wore a blue silk dress, a wonderful coat to match, blue shoes and socks, and a hat that was so full of flowers it looked like a little garden.

It was the hat that everyone admired so much. There were daisies, buttercups, cornflowers, poppies and grass round the hat, and it suited Clara perfectly. She knew this, so she always wore her hat, even when she played games with the toys.

"You are vain, Clara!" said the teddy bear teasingly.

That made Clara go red. She *was* vain, and she knew she was pretty.

She knew that her clothes were lovely. She knew that her flowery hat was the prettiest one the toys had ever seen, and that it made her look really sweet.

"I'm not vain!" said Clara. "Not a bit!"

"You are! You're conceited and stuck-up," said the teddy bear, who always said what he thought. "You even wear

your hat when you play with us. And if we play a bit roughly you turn up your nose and say, 'Oh, please! You'll tear my pretty frock!' Pooh! Conceited Clara!"

Clara was angry. She glared at the bear and then she walked straight up to him. She took hold of his pink bow and tugged at it. It came undone, and Clara pulled it off. And then she tore the ribbon in half. Wasn't she naughty?

"Oh! You horrid doll! Look what you've done! You've torn my ribbon and now I can't tie it round my neck, and I shall show where my head is sewn on to my body," wept the bear.

"Serves you right," said Clara, and she walked off.

Well, after that the toys wouldn't have anything to do with Clara. They wouldn't play with her. They wouldn't talk to her. They wouldn't even speak when she called to them. So Clara was cross and unhappy.

One night, when the children were asleep and the toys came alive to play, Clara took her beautiful flowery hat and hung it up in the dolls' house. She thought perhaps the toys might play with her if she didn't wear her hat. She fluffed out her curly hair and gazed at the teddy bear.

"Ho!" said the bear. "Now you want to show off your curly hair, I suppose! Well, go and show it somewhere else! *We* don't want to see it, Conceited Clara!"

So that wasn't any use. Clara went to a corner and sulked. She was very angry. How dare the toys take no notice of her, the prettiest doll in the whole nursery!

Then the toys planned a party. It was the birthday of the clockwork mouse, and everyone loved him because he was such a dear. So they thought they would have a party for him and games, and give him a lovely time.

But they didn't ask Clara. The teddy

cooked some exciting cakes and biscuits on the stove in the dolls' house, and cut up a rosy apple into slices. The toys set out the chairs round the little wooden table and put the dishes and plates ready.

Everything looked so nice. "It's a pity that we can't put a vase of flowers in the middle of the table," said the teddy bear. "I always think flowers look so sweet at a party. Come along, everyone – we'll just go and tidy ourselves up and then the party can begin."

They all went to find the brush and comb in the toy-cupboard. Clara peeped from her corner and thought that the birthday-table looked lovely with its cakes and biscuits and apple-slices.

"I do wish I had something to give the clockwork mouse," thought Clara. "I do love him. He's such a dear. But I expect he would throw it back at me if I had anything to give. The toys are all so horrid to me now."

And then Clara suddenly had a

marvellous idea. What about her flowery hat? Couldn't she take the flowers off that beautiful hat and put them into a vase for the middle of the birthday-table? They would look really lovely.

She rushed to get her hat. She tore the flowers from it. She found a dear little vase, and began to put them in – buttercups, daisies, cornflowers, poppies and grass. You can't think how sweet they looked.

Clara popped the vase of flowers in the middle of the table and went back to her corner. She looked at her hat rather sadly. It looked very odd without its flowers. She would look funny if she wore it any more.

The toys ran to the birthday-table to begin the party – and how they stared when they saw the lovely flowers in the middle of the table!

"Where did they come from?" cried the teddy bear in astonishment.

"Oh, what a lovely surprise for me!"

cried the clockwork mouse. And then he guessed who had put the flowers there for him.

"It's Clara! They are the flowers out of her hat!" he squeaked. "Oh, Clara, thank you! Do, do come to my party!"

"Yes, do come!" cried all the toys. And the bear ran and took her hand.

"If you can give up the flowers you were so proud of, you can't be so horrid after all!" he cried. "Come along, Clara, and join the party."

So Clara went, and everyone was so nice to her that she was quite happy again. Sometimes she wears her hat without the flowers, and do you know what the toys say? They say, "Why, Clara, you look just as nice without the flowers – you really do!"

And so she does!

Mother Hubbard's honey

Mother Hubbard kept bees, and they made lovely golden honey for her. Mother Hubbard took it from the hives and put it into jars.

Then her cupboard was full when she went to it, instead of bare. Rows upon rows of honey jars stood there, waiting to be sold.

Now little Pixie Peep-About lived next door to Mother Hubbard, and he loved honey. But he wasn't a very good or very helpful pixie, so Mother Hubbard didn't give him any honey. She sold most of it, gave some to her friends, and kept six pots for herself.

Pixie Peep-About was cross because she never gave him any honey. "And I

live next door, too!" he said to himself.
"She might have given me just a taste.
She knows I love honey."

But Peep-About never gave Mother
Hubbard any of his gooseberries when

they were ripe. And he didn't offer her an egg when his hens laid plenty. So it wasn't surprising that he didn't get any honey.

One summer he watched Mother Hubbard's bees.

"How busy they are!" he said, as he peeped over the wall. "In and out, in and out of those hives all the day long. And what is more, a lot of those bees come into *my* garden and take the honey from *my* flowers!"

It was quite true. They did. But bees go anywhere and everywhere, so of course they went into Peep-About's garden too.

"Some of that honey they are storing in Mother Hubbard's hives is mine, taken from my flowers," thought Peep-About. "So Mother Hubbard ought to give me plenty!"

He told Mother Hubbard this, but she laughed. "Honey is free in the flowers!" she said. "Don't be silly, Peep-About."

Now, one day Mother Hubbard went

to take the honeycombs from her hives.
They were beautiful combs, full of
golden honey. She meant to separate
the honey from the combs, and store
it in her jars. Peep-About knew she
was going to do that. She did it every
year.

"Now she'll have jars upon jars of
honey, and she won't give me a single
one," thought the pixie. "It's too bad.
I haven't tasted honey for months,
and I should love some on bread and
butter."

Mother Hubbard poured the honey
into her jars. She handed one to old
Mister Potter, at the bottom of the
garden. He was a kind old fellow, and
always gave Mother Hubbard tomatoes
when he had some to spare. He was
delighted.

"Look at that now!" said Peep-About
to himself. "Not a drop for me! Mean
old thing! My, what delicious honey it
looked!"

The next day Mother Hubbard

dressed herself up in her best coat and hat, and set out to catch the bus, with three pots of honey in her basket. Peep-About met her as she went to the bus.

"Where are you going?" asked Peep-About.

"To see my sister, Dame Blue-Bonnet," said Mother Hubbard. "I'll be gone all day, so if you see the milkman, Peep-About, tell him to leave me a pint of milk."

"Gone all day!" thought Peep-About. "Well, what about me getting in at the kitchen window, going to that cupboard, and helping myself to a few spoonfuls of honey!"

So, when Mother Hubbard had safely got on the bus, Peep-About crept in at her kitchen window and went to the cupboard. It wasn't locked. He opened it, and saw row upon row of jars of honey. Oh, what a lovely sight!

He was small and the cupboard was high. He tried to scramble up to one of the shelves, and he upset a jar of honey. Down it went, and poured all over him!

"Gracious!" said Peep-About in alarm. "It's all over me! How lovely it tastes!"

He thought he had better go into his own home, scrape the honey off himself, and eat it that way. So out of the window he went.

But the garden was full of Mother Hubbard's bees, and they smelt the honey on Peep-About at once.

"Zzzzzz! Honey! ZZZZZZZ! Honey!" they buzzed to one another, and flew round Peep-About. They tried to settle on the honey that was running down his head and neck.

"Go away! Go away! Stop buzzing round me!" he cried. But no matter how he waved them away, they came back again.

And now Peep-About had a terrible time, for wherever he went the bees went too. They followed him into his kitchen. They stung him when he flapped them away. They followed him out into the garden again. They followed him into the street. They wouldn't leave Peep-About alone for one minute.

He couldn't sit down and have his dinner. He had to go without his tea. He ran here and he ran there, but always the bees flew with him.

He had their honey on him, and they wanted it.

More and more bees came to join in the fun. At last Peep-About saw Mother Hubbard walking up her front path and he ran to her. She was astonished to see her bees round him in a big buzzing cloud.

"Take them away! Make them go to their hive!" wept Peep-About.

Mother Hubbard touched him and found he was sticky with honey. Then she knew what had happened.

"You went to steal some of my honey," she said, sternly. "You're a bad pixie. You can keep the honey – and the bees too! I shan't call them off!"

So, until the bees went to bed in their hive that night, poor Peep-About had to put up with them. He ran for miles trying to get rid of them, but he couldn't. They could fly faster than he could run!

At last the bees went to bed.

Peep-About stripped off his sticky suit and washed it. He got himself a meal. He cried all the time. "I shall never like honey again," he wept. "Never, never, never!"

Mother Hubbard was sorry the next day that she hadn't helped poor Peep-About, even though he had been a bad little pixie. So she sent him a tiny jar of honey all for himself.

But wasn't it a pity – he couldn't eat it! He didn't like honey any more. He couldn't bear to look at it.

"It serves me right!" he said. "When I couldn't have it, I loved it, and tried to take it. Now, here I've got a jar, and I can't bear to eat it. It's a good punishment for me, it really is!"